Laughter is Good Medicine

Doc's Silly Clean "Groaner" Jokes

Sammy Silly Joke

Silly clean jokes for you and your family!

JAMES A. SURRELL, M.D.

"THERE ISN'T MUCH HUMOR IN MEDICINE,
BUT THERE IS A LOT OF MEDICINE IN HUMOR."

Laughter is Good Medicine!
Doc's Silly Clean
"Groaner" Jokes

by James A. Surrell, M.D.

Published by
BEAN BOOKS, LLC, Newberry, Michigan
sosdietdoc@gmail.com

Designed by Stacey Willey
Cover and Illustrations by Stephanie Lake

ISBN # 978-0-9825601-4-3

Table of Contents

Introduction and Medical Benefits of Laughter and Smiling

First, I must let you know that I never will tell, nor do I ever want to hear, any of the so called "dirty jokes." If I can't tell the joke to a third grader, then I really do not want to hear it. I must also let you know that for some unknown reason, I rarely forget a joke that someone tells me. Based on the fact that most of my jokes are referred to as "Groaners", a lot of my colleagues and friends wish I would forget most of my jokes, but sorry, I always seem to be able to remember these silly clean jokes. Over the years of telling so many silly jokes, I often get this reply, "Doc, that's the dumbest joke I have ever heard." But I have now learned what they truly mean by this comment, as follows. "Wow, Doc, I really hope I can remember that bad joke, so I can tell my friends and co-workers and get them groaning as much as I did." You may note that a few of the jokes are repeated, as they may fit into more than one of my joke categories.

LAUGHTER HEALTH BENEFITS – We have all heard the term that "Laughter is Good Medicine", and this is certainly true. This is not just someone's opinion as there have been numerous scientific studies that have, indeed, confirmed this to be a medically proven fact. Let's now take a brief look at what laughter can do for all of us.

The following information has been reported by the United States National Library of Medicine. First, where does laughter come from? Our laughter is stimulated from two different sources. Most of our laughter would be considered spontaneous laughter that is triggered by an external source. That is, we laugh at something that we heard or saw, or somebody says or does something that makes us laugh. This would be our reaction to seeing a good comedy show or hearing a comedian that we thought was really funny. The second and much less common source of our laughter comes from within. This laughter is triggered by our thinking of or recalling something that just makes us laugh.

With regard to whether our laughter is triggered from an outside source, or from within, the brain is not able to distinguish between these two sources. Therefore, scientists who have studied laughter believe that similar benefits occur, regardless of the source of the laughter. They also conclude that the benefits of laughter are many.

Here are just some of the beneficial side-effects of laughter. Laughter has been shown to offer physiological, psychological, social, spiritual, and overall quality-of-life benefits. There really are no negative effects of laughter and it should go without saying that laughter is really good for us. Scientifically speaking, there are absolutely no medical reasons not to laugh.

Numerous medical specialists have studied the effects of humor with regard to medicine and healing. They all agree that laughter does provide multiple healthy benefits. First, it is clear that laughter can be a great form of stress relief. As more and more scientific studies are being done to look at the effects of laughter and one's health, the evidence continues to mount confirming the many positive things that laughter can do for all of us. For example, when we have a good laugh, we tend to breathe more deeply so you take in more oxygen and this stimulates your lungs, your heart, and your muscles. Laughter can also stimulate circulation and this will help with muscle relaxation, which helps reduce many of the physical symptoms of stress. Laughter may also ease pain by causing the body to produce its own natural painkillers, known as endorphins.

SMILING HEALTH BENEFITS – I truly believe that many of us underestimate the positive impact a simple smile may have when we interact with others. Of course, a smile is non-verbal, but it can truly carry a very strong positive message to the person or persons to whom it is directed. Let's now take a look at some of the impact a simple smile may have on a person that has a true smile sent their way.

First, take a look at my top ten profound quotes that certainly tell us very much about smiles.

1. "We shall never know all the good that a simple smile can do." Saint Mother Teresa

2. "A warm smile is the universal language of kindness." William Arthur Ward

3. "A gentle word, a kind look, a good-natured smile can work wonders and accomplish miracles." William Hazlitt

4. "A smile is the light in your window that tells others that there is a caring, sharing person inside." Denis Waitley

5. "Smile in the mirror. Do that every morning and you'll start to see a big difference in your life." Yoko Ono

6. "A smile is happiness you'll find right under your nose." Tom Wilson

7. "Most smiles are started by another smile." Frank A. Clark

8. "Wear a smile and have friends; wear a scowl and have wrinkles." George Eliot

9. "I have witnessed the softening of the hardest of hearts by a simple smile." Goldie Hawn

10. "Nothing you wear is more important than your smile." Connie Stevens

Let us now take a brief look at some of the science and human physiology about our smiles. Following is a common definition of a human "smile." A smile is a facial expression formed primarily by flexing the muscles at the sides of the mouth. Further, a true smile will also include a contraction of the muscles at the corner of the eyes. It is well accepted that a genuine human smile is truly an expression that shows pleasure, sociability, happiness, joy, or amusement.

So, what are the biological benefits of smiling? According to "Psychology Today" magazine, smiling activates the release of our natural human neurotransmitters within our body that work toward fighting off stress. These neurotransmitters are chemical agents that serve as messengers within the human brain. Our internal "feel good" neurotransmitters, including dopamine, endorphins and serotonin, are all released when a smile flashes across our face. Therefore, this simple act of smiling will serve to relax our body, and can also lower our heart rate and reduce our blood pressure.

The bottom line is that a simple human smile has a truly significant effect on our brain chemistry. When we smile, this causes endorphins and other internal brain chemicals to be released. The action of these brain chemicals will help reduce any internal tension we may be feeling. They will also help us deal with other outside stressful situations that we may be experiencing. Now, don't just sit there, give me a smile!

Chapter 1 – Animal, Fish, Bird, and Hunting Jokes

Animal Jokes

What did mama buffalo say to her son when he left to go off to school? "Bison!"

Why did the turtle cross the road? He was going to the Shell station.

Why did the turtle need to go to the Shell station? He ran out of "Turtle Wax."

Why did the race horse cross the road? He was looking for "fast" food.

Why shouldn't ponies give speeches? Because they are a little "hoarse."

Who is the penguin's favorite relative? His "Aunt Arctica."

What is black and white and red all over? An embarrassed zebra.

What do you call a bear with no teeth? A gummy bear.

What do you call a bear in the middle of a thunderstorm? A "Drizzly Bear.

What do you call a deer in the middle of a thunderstorm? A "Rain Deer."

What do you call a polar bear in the middle of the Sahara desert? Lost.

Why is an elephant like a Volkswagen Beetle? They both have their trunk in the front.

What is as big as an elephant and doesn't weigh even one ounce? His shadow.

What do you call a dog stuck in a snow bank? A chilly dog.

What do you call new-born puppies before they learn how to bark? Hush Puppies.

What is the reptiles favorite movie? "The Lizard of Oz."

Fish Jokes

What is the most patriotic fish in the USA? Uncle Salmon.

What is the best way to communicate with a fish? Just drop him a line!

Cook a man a fish and you feed him for a day. But teach a man to fish and you can get rid of him for a whole weekend.

What do you get when you cross a banker with a fish? A loan shark.

What do sea monsters eat? Fish and ships.

What did the fish say when he swam into a wall? Dam! What kind of fish would swim into the wall? A walleye.

Why do fish never graduate and get out of school? Because their grades are always below "Sea Level."

Where do fish sleep? In their water bed.

Where do fish keep their money? In the River Bank.

Why have you never seen a fish with a cold? Because every day they take Vitamin "Sea."

What happened to the shark when he swallowed a bunch of keys? He got lockjaw!

What kind of fish prefers to only come out at night? The Starfish.

Big brother fish told this to baby brother fish. Keep your mouth shut & you won't get caught.

Which kind of fish lives up in a tree? A perch.

Which day of the week really scares fish? Fry-day.

Bird Jokes

Why do seagulls only fly around the sea? Because if they flew around the bay, they would be called bay-gulls (bagels).

How do veterinarians treat sick birds? They give them the proper "tweetment."

Why did the turkey cross the road? Because it was the chicken's day off.

A chicken was seen dancing in the chicken coupe. It truly was "poultry in motion."

Why did the chicken cross the road? To prove to the raccoon that it actually could be done.

The rooster crossed the road, jumped in a big mud puddle, got all muddy, and then came back across the road. He turned out to be a "Dirty Double Crosser."

Canadian Geese always fly in a large "V Formation." Why is one side on the "V" longer than the other side? Because there are more geese on that side.

Why does a chicken coop have only 2 doors? If it had 4 doors, it would be a chicken sedan.

If a rooster laid an egg in the pond, would it sink or float? Neither, because roosters don't lay eggs.

Which bird cannot control itself and never stop eating? The swallow.

What do ducks really like to eat with their cheese? "Quackers."

Which type of bird really likes to hang around construction sites? The crane.

Why do humming birds hum? Because they can't remember the words.

Who is the penguin's favorite relative? His "Aunt Arctica."

What is the penguin's favorite song to sing? "Freeze a jolly good fellow."

Hunting Jokes

Two hunters were driving out to their hunting camp to hunt for bears and they saw a sign that said, "Bear Left." So, they turned around and went back home.

Most guys refer to it as "Deer Camp." Most ladies more accurately refer to it as "Beer Camp."

One first time deer hunter saw some tracks and he got excited and started to follow them. His hunting buddy saw him and advised him that you do not need to follow train tracks.

What do you call a deer with no eyes? No Eye Deer. Where does the deer with no eyes live? In his "Deer Blind."

What did the bird hunter ask for on his birthday? A birthday pheasant.

One hunter asked another, "Have you ever hunted bear?" The other hunter replied, "No, I always wear clothes and my hunting vest."

What is the difference between a hunter and a fisherman? A hunter lies in wait, whereas a fisherman waits and lies.

Two skunks were out in the forest and they saw a hunter with his rifle coming toward them. One skunk then said to the other skunk, "I think it's time for us to kneel down and start to spray."

A dog breeder crossed a hunting dog with a telephone. He got a Golden Receiver.

When the hunter left for deer camp, he promised his wife he would bring back some venison. On the way back from his unsuccessful hunting trip he stopped at the grocery store and asked for some venison. The butcher told him all he had was some hamburger. The hunter replied, "That won't work because she'll think I shot a cow."

What is the definition of a very rare and well-informed deer? One that stays off the highway.

Chapter 2 – Dog and Cat Jokes

What dog always knows what time it is? A watch dog.

What do dogs have in common with cell phones? They both have collar I.D.

Why are cats afraid of trees? Because of the "bark."

Why can't dogs and cats dance very well? Because they all have two left feet.

What do you call a dog with no legs? You don't call him… he won't come anyway.

Where do you find a dog with no legs? Right where you left him.

Why did the dog cross the road? To get to the "barking" lot.

What is the name of the dog who is a great detective? Sherlock Bones.

What is the Dracula's favorite dog breed? Dracula really likes blood hounds.

What is the cat's favorite breakfast food? Mice Krispies.

What is the favorite dessert of every cat? A mice cream cone.

What is the difference between a cat and a comma? A cat has claws at the end of its paws, but a comma is a pause at the end of a clause.

What do you call a cat that loves to go bowling? An alley cat.

What did the Dalmatian dog say after he ate his favorite dog food? Now, that really hit the spots.

What did one flea ask the other flea? "Should we walk, or just take the dog?"

What market should the dog never, ever go to? The flea market.

Every season is
silly joke season!

Chapter 3 – Autumn, Winter, and Spring Jokes

Autumn (Fall) Jokes

What did the boy autumn leaf say to the lovely girl autumn leaf? I'm really falling for you.

Why do Northern Michigan birds fly south to Florida in the Fall? Because it's way too far to walk.

If money really did grow on trees, in the Fall we would all be raking it in.

How do trees get onto the internet? It's easy for them because they just "log" on.

Why was Summer able to catch up with Autumn? Because Autumn had a "Fall."

Why do trees dislike going back to school in the Fall? Because they are easily "stumped."

What is the best vehicle to use for your Fall hay ride? Your "Autumn-mobile."

What do trees say when their leaves grow back in the Spring? What a "re-leaf."

A friend of mine got tired of looking at all those leaves in his yard, so he took action. He got off the couch and closed the curtains.

When Summer is out and Autumn is in, we go from swimming pools to football pools.

Fall is that time of year to drag out your Winter clothes and see what fun the moths had in your closet all Summer long.

Humpty Dumpty had a great Fall. And I sincerely hope you always do, too.

Winter Jokes

One snowman looked at the neighbor snowman in the front yard next to him, and he asked the other snowman, "Do you smell carrots?"

What do you call two straight days of 10 to 12 inches of heavy blinding white-out snow in Michigan's Upper Peninsula? The week-end.

What is the name of Mr. Snowman's favorite aunt? Aunt Arctica. What is the name of Mr. Snowman's least favorite uncle? Uncle Sunny.

Snowmen prefer to use "cold" cash, but if they run out of cash, they go take money out of their account at the "Snow Bank."

One winter day it was so cold that the politicians kept their hands in their own pockets. The next day it was even colder so the politicians started blowing even more hot air.

Last week's cold spell was almost as cold as lying down on the hospital x-ray table.

How do you scare a snowman? Just show him your hair dryer.

Why do you primarily see only Snowmen, and you don't see a Snow Woman? It's because only us men are dumb enough to go stay outside without a coat.

The snowman really likes to go for a ride on his ice-cycle!

What did the winter hat say to the winter scarf? "You just hang around down there, because I am going on a head."

Why did the snowman climb the mountain? He was looking for his "ice cap."

The snowman's favorite breakfast is Frosted Flakes and his favorite lunch is icebergers.

What do you call a snowman on roller blades? A snowmobile.

What is the snow lady's favorite cosmetic? She loves cold cream.

What is another name for winter ice on the roads in Northern Michigan? Skid Stuff.

Mrs. Penguin sent Mr. Penguin out to purchase some bedding for their new igloo. He shopped all around the North Pole and came back with "sheets of ice and blankets of snow." She was thrilled with his shopping choices.

Spring Jokes

Why is everybody so tired on April 1st? Because we all just completed a 31 day March.

You know for sure it is the first day of Spring in Michigan's Upper Peninsula because you can now start to see over some of the snow banks.

If April showers bring May flowers, what do May flowers bring? Pilgrims.

What keeps falling down but never gets hurt? The Spring raindrops.

What goes up when the rain comes down? Your umbrella.

What do you call it when it rains chickens and ducks? That is really FOWL weather.

What kind of bow can never be tied? A rain-bow.

What did the Summer say to the Spring? Help! I'm going to Fall.

What do you get when you plant chocolate candy kisses in your Spring time garden? Tulips (two lips).

Why did the farmer bury all his money out in his field? To be sure that his soil was rich.

What can be seen right in the middle of the months of April and March, that can never be seen at the beginning or at the end of these two months? The letter "r."

Why is the letter "A" like a Spring flower? Because a bee "B" always comes right after it.

Why did the farmer plant seeds in his pond? He was trying to grow "water" melons.

Spring is that time of year to drag out your Summer clothes to see if they still fit, or to find out how much they may have "shrunk."

When is the best season for people to start using their trampoline? "Spring" time.

Chapter 4 – Holiday Jokes

Valentine's Day, St. Patrick's Day, Easter, Fourth of July, Halloween, Thanksgiving, Christmas

Valentine's Day Jokes

I asked a lady if she had a date for Valentine's Day. She replied, "Yes, it's February 14th."

She then told me she could not go out with me because of an illness. I asked her, "What is your illness?" She relied, "Doc, your jokes make me sick!"

I then decided to give her a Valentine flower. I gave her a cauliflower.

St. Patrick's Day Irish Jokes

How do you get an Irishman to go up on the roof? Tell him the drinks are on the house.

When is an Irish Potato not Irish? When it's a French Fry!

I asked an Irish Leprechaun to loan me $5.00. He said he couldn't because he was a little short.

What position does the leprechaun play on the Irish baseball team? Shortstop, of course!

What do you get when you cross poison ivy with a 4-leaf clover? A rash of good luck.

Why should you never iron a wrinkled 4-leaf clover? Because you would truly be pressing your luck!

What is Irish and lives in your back yard all summer long? Patty O'furniture.

How can you tell if an Irishman is having a good time? He's "Dublin" over with laughter!

How did the Irish Jig get started? Too much green beer and not enough restrooms!

Two Irishman, Paddy and Mick, were walking home from the Irish pub. Paddy had a bag of Irish potatoes in his hand. Paddy said to Mick, "If you can guess how many potatoes are in my bag, you can have them both."

A leprechaun saw a very tall laughing man wearing green. It was the Jolly Green Giant.

What do you call a great big Irish spider? Paddy long legs.

An Irishman walked out of a bar. Well, you know, it could happen…

Easter Bunny Jokes

Why did the Easter Bunny cross the road? He was going to IHOP for breakfast.

Why did the Lady Easter Bunny hop across the road? She was going to her "Hare" Dresser.

What do you call an Easter Bunny with fleas? The "Fleaster Bunny."

What do you call a bunch of rabbits hopping backwards across the road? A receding hare line.

What do you call the Easter Bunny when he tells good jokes? A funny bunny.

What is the Easter Bunny's favorite dance? It would have to be the Bunny Hop.

Do bunnies use combs? No, they use hare brushes.

What is the favorite music of bunny rabbits? Hip Hop!

Which bunnies were famous bank robbers? Bunny and Clyde.

What is the favorite game that little bunnies love to play? Hopscotch.

Why was the lady bunny so upset? She was having a bad "hare" day!

Carrots must be are really good for your eyes, because you never see a bunny rabbit wearing glasses.

Fourth of July Jokes

Following is what I truly believe should be the Official Fourth of July fish? "Uncle Salmon."

What did General Washington say to his men before they crossed the Delaware River? Get in the boat!

What is red, white, black and blue? Uncle Sam after he fell off the float in the 4th of July parade.

What is red, white, blue, and yellow? The Star Spangled Banana!

Why is Santa Claus like the American flag? They both hang out at a pole!

What kind of tea were the American colonists willing to fight for? "Liber-tea."

What do you call a cracker covered with Tabasco Hot Sauce? A Fire Cracker!

What is another very patriotic United States fish? It would be a Red, White and Bluegill.

Why did our Founding Fathers truly live like ants? Because they lived in colonies.

What did one flag say to the other flag on the Fourth of July? It didn't say anything, it just waved.

What did the other flag say back? Quit waving at me. I came out here to "hang out" alone.

Doc Surrell told one of his bad groaner jokes to the Liberty Bell? He really cracked it up!

Halloween Jokes

How much did the Halloween pirate pay to have his ears pierced? A Buccaneer!

How do you fix a hole in a pumpkin? Use a pumpkin patch!

Which side of the pumpkin should you put the face on? The outside!

Why was the skeleton afraid to cross the road? Because he had no guts!

Why did the skeleton want to cross the road? He was looking for a "body" shop.

Why did the Halloween skeleton go to the grocery store? To get some "spare ribs."

What happened when the Halloween witch's broom failed & she crashed on the beach? She became a sand-witch!

What is the favorite dessert of the Halloween ghost? I scream!

What do moms dress up as on Halloween? Mummies!

What does the Halloween witch use to keep her hair in place? Scare spray!

What do you get when you cross a snowman with a vampire? Frostbite.

Why do you never see Halloween witches as identical twins? Because you would not be able to tell which Witch was which!

Why is the Halloween skeleton so mean? Because he has no heart.

What do vampires take when they have a bad cough? Coffin drops!

What do you get when you cross a duck with a vampire? Count Quackula!

Thanksgiving Jokes

What do you call an impolite obnoxious turkey? Dinner.

What's the best dance to do on Thanksgiving? The turkey trot.

Why did they welcome the turkey to join the band? Because he had the drumsticks.

If April showers bring May flowers, what do Mayflowers bring? Pilgrims.

Why did the Pastor kick the turkey out of church? Because he kept using "Fowl" language.

Why did the Police arrest the Thanksgiving turkey? He was engaged in "Fowl" play!

Why did they kick the turkey off the baseball team? Because he could only hit "Fowl" balls.

Where does the turkey go to eat with his duck friends? The "Quacker" Barrel restaurant.

Why was the Thanksgiving soup so expensive? It was a "24 carrot" soup.

What happened when the turkey got into a fight? He got the stuffing knocked out of him!

Which side of the turkey has the most feathers? The outside.

Little Johnny's teacher asked him to write a paper about: "What I'm thankful for on Thanksgiving," He wrote, "I am thankful that I'm not a turkey." The teacher gave him an "A."

Christmas Jokes

What is the favorite subject of Santa's Elves in school? Of course, it would be the ELF-abet.

What nationality is Santa Claus? North Polish.

What do you call an elf who sings while he wraps Christmas presents? A Christmas "wrapper."

What do you call people who are afraid of Santa Claus? Claus-trophobic.

What do you call an impolite obnoxious reindeer? RUDEolph.

Why was Santa's little helper depressed? Because he had low "elf" esteem.

Santa Claus asked Mrs. Claus on Christmas Eve, "What does the weather look like?" Mrs. Claus replied, "It looks like "Rain-Dear."

What do you call a kid who doesn't believe in Santa? A rebel without a Claus.

What is red, white, and black and blue? Santa Claus, after he fell out of his sleigh.

Following are the four medical stages of man's life:

1. You believe in Santa Claus

2. You don't believe in Santa Claus

3. You dress up as Santa Claus

4. You look like Santa Claus

Chapter 5 – Clean Church Jokes

Why did Moses spent 40 years roaming around the desert? Because he was a guy and he wouldn't stop and ask for directions.

The Sunday School teacher asked the young kids in her class why they should all be very quiet when they return to the church after their Sunday School class. Little Mary Ann raised her hand and answered, "Because most of the people are asleep."

Why did Noah not allow any fishing off the ark? Because he only had two worms.

Why didn't God have Jesus born in Washington, D.C.? He couldn't find three Wise Men.

Did Eve ever have a date with Adam? No, they just had an apple.

Why should the man of the house always make the coffee for the lady of the house? Because the Bible says, "Hebrews."

Where is the practice of medicine first seen in the Bible? It was when God gave Moses two tablets.

What do you call a sleepwalking nun? That would certainly be a "Roamin' Catholic."

What is the favorite fish of most Priests and Pastors? Holy Mackerel.

If God is your Co-pilot, then I would strongly recommend that you swap seats.

What is the first name of the man who will never sit or stand in church? Neil.

With regard to your prayers, know that God will always answer your "knee-mail."

The church welcomes all denominations – fives, tens, twenties, fifties…

Sammy
Silly
Joke

Laughter is good medicine! ➔

Chapter 6 – Nurse, Doctor, Dentist, and Pharmacist Jokes

Nurse Jokes

What do you call a doctor who does not listen to the nursing staff? Unenlightened, inexperienced, and in deep trouble!

What advice did the experienced nurse give to the student nurse as she was about to give her first penicillin injection? Just give it your "best shot."

What is it called when the hospital runs out of maternity ward nurses? That would be a "Mid-Wife" crisis.

What is the primary thing that really upsets organ transplant nurses? Rejection.

What's the difference between a Nurse and a Nun? A Nun only has to serve one God.

How many nurses does it take to change a light bulb? None, the student nurse does it.

The nursing students all brought red magic markers to their first hospital training session because they were told they might have to "draw" blood.

Recent nursing school graduates want everyone to know they are a nurse. Experienced nurses don't want anyone to know they are a nurse.

Here is a major difference between a student nurse and an experienced nurse. A student nurse throws up when the patient throws up. The experienced nurse just calls housekeeping.

You likely are an experienced nurse if when using a public restroom, you wash your hands for a least a full minute, and then turn off the faucets with your elbows.

The nurse asked the first year medical student if he took the patient's temperature. The medical student replied, "No, is it missing?"

Many nurses on one floor became ill at the same time. It truly was a "staff" infection.

Doctor Jokes

Today I could not decide if I was Mickey Mouse or if I was Donald Duck. So, I went to the Emergency Room and they told me not to worry. I was just having a "Disney Spell."

A patient came to see me and said, "Doc, you have to help me - I broke my leg in two places!" So, I advised him, "Don't ever go back to those places."

A patient came to see me and told me his memory was no good. I told him: "Forget it."

What is the difference between a new young puppy dog and a doctor? Well, eventually the new young puppy dog will grow up and stop whining!

A patient came to see me and said, "Doc, you have to

help me. Nobody, and I mean nobody, pays any attention to me!" So I said, "Next."

How many Psychiatrists does it take to change a light bulb? Well, it just takes one… but the light bulb has to really want to change.

Three men died in a car accident and met St. Peter at the Heavenly Gates. St. Peter asked each of them about their life on earth. The first man told St. Peter he was a minister and he went right in. The second man told St. Peter he was a kindergarten teacher and he went right in. The third man advised St. Peter he was an HMO President, and St. Peter said he could go in, but he could only stay 3 days.

Why does it take one million sperm to fertilize just one egg? Because the sperm are men and they won't stop and ask for directions.

A nurse came rushing in to my exam room and told me that my patient out in the waiting room had just turned invisible! So I told her to tell him I can't see him today!

I recently did hemorrhoid surgery on a patient. He wrote me a check to pay for the surgery. Later I called him and told him, "We have a problem here because your check came back." He said, "Well, that makes us even Doc, because so did my hemorrhoids."

Here is the proof that diarrhea is hereditary. It runs in your jeans.

Dentist Jokes

What is the absolute best time to go to your dentist? When it's "tooth hurty" (2:30).

Why did the Queen go to see her dentist? She wanted to get a new "crown."

I went to my dentist with an abscessed tooth and a severe toothache. She saw me right away and said, "Don't worry, I will get right to the root of the problem."

You don't have to brush all of your teeth, just the ones you want to keep. In other words, ignore your teeth and they will all go away.

What did the judge say to the dentist? "Do you swear to pull the tooth, the whole tooth and nothing but the tooth?"

Why are false teeth like the stars? Because they both only come out at night.

What are the six most scary words for a 10 year old? The dentist will see you now.

Pharmacist Jokes

What do you call a pharmacist working at the veterinary drug store? A "farm-assist."

A pharmacist just told me that the definition of a "miracle drug" is one that is still the same price as it was last year.

How many pharmacists does it take to change a light bulb? It just takes one, but you have to do it three times a day for 10 days.

A man goes into a drugstore and asks the pharmacist if she can give him something for the hiccups. The pharmacist promptly reaches out and she slaps the man's face. "What did you do that for?" the man yells. "Well, you don't have the hiccups anymore, do you?" "No," the man replies, "but my wife out in the car still does!"

A pharmacist is going over the directions on the prescription bottle with a new customer and tells the customer, "Be sure not to take this medication more often than every 4 hours." The customer then replies, "Don't worry, it takes me about 4 hours to get the lid off the bottle."

Chapter 7 – Automobile, Motorcycle and Bicycle Jokes

Automobile Jokes

It may be time to trade in your vehicle if the Blue Book value of your old pick-up truck goes up and down depending on how much gas is in it.

A set of car jumper cables crawled into a bar. The bartender looked down at the jumper cables and told them, "Don't you start anything in here!"

What is the official scientific medical name for a car salesman? A "car deal-ologist."

A friend told me he gave up his seat to a blind person on a bus. He then told me that was how he lost his job as the bus driver.

A wife got a new car for her husband. She said it was a great trade and she loves her new car.

We all know that women are very good at multi-tasking and that men are not so good at it. However, I just figured out the one true multi-tasking activity that most of us men can do. Most of us can drive our car and listen to the radio at the same time.

Confucius say, man who runs behind a car will get "exhausted."

Who earns a living by actually driving their customers away? That would be a taxi driver.

The very best way to get back on your feet is to miss a couple of your car payments.

It is likely time to buy a new car if you park your car, leave the keys in the ignition, leave it unlocked, and have no worry about it ever being stolen.

A friend of mine told me he just paid off three cars. One for his doctor, one for his dentist, and one for his lawyer.

My old used car offers me a religious experience. Every morning I pray that it will start.

My friend's car is so old that it had to have cataract surgery on its headlights.

Motorcycle Jokes

Why did the motorcycle fall asleep? Because it was "Two Tired."

The best view of a thunderstorm from your Harley Davidson is in your rear view mirror.

Only bikers truly understand why dogs love to stick their heads out of car windows.

A bike on the road is worth two in the shop.

When you are the lead rider, don't spit.

Don't ever argue with an 18-wheeler.

There are old bikers and there are some drunk bikers, but there are no old drunk bikers.

If you decide to ride your motorcycle crazy like there's no tomorrow, there won't be.

Gray-haired bikers didn't get that way from pure luck.

You'll know she truly loves you if she offers to let you ride her new Harley Davidson. Don't do it and she'll love you even more.

Keep your bike in good repair, because your motorcycle boots are not comfortable for walking.

Here is my profound medical motorcycle advice – never ride faster than your Guardian Angel can fly.

Bicycle Jokes

What is the hardest thing about learning to ride your bicycle? The pavement.

If you ride without your helmet, you won't hurt your brain, because you don't have one.

If you decide to ride your bike crazy in heavy traffic, you may turn into a hood ornament.

What do you get when you cross a bicycle with a rose? You get bicycle petals.

How did the kid bicycle refer to his daddy bicycle? He's my "Pop-cycle."

Your bicycle on the road is worth two in your garage.

Why did the boy take his bicycle to bed? Because he didn't want to walk in his sleep.

Elephants should never ride bikes because they have no thumb to ring the bell.

A man went bankrupt and could no longer ride his bike because he lost all his balance.

Dracula rode his bike around scaring people. He named his bike the "vicious cycle."

Sammy
Silly
Joke

Be sure to drive and ride safe!

Chapter 8 – Sport and Golf Jokes

Sport Jokes

What did the football coach say to the broken vending machine? Give me my quarterback!

Why do coaches like punters? Because punters always put their best foot forward.

What did the football say to the punter? I really get a kick out of you.

Why didn't the dog want to play football? Because he was a boxer.

Why didn't the skeleton try out for the football team? His heart just wasn't in it.

What do football wide receivers catch after running downfield? Their breath.

Why did the turkey get kicked out of the basketball game? For fowl play.

What do hockey players and a magician have in common? They both love to do hat tricks.

What stories are told by professional NBA basketball players? Tall stories.

Why do basketball players love their cookies? Because they can dunk them.

What is the proof the elephants truly love the sport of swimming? They never leave home without their trunks.

Why was the police officer called to come to the baseball game? Because somebody stole second base.

Golf Jokes

People often ask me, "Doc, why did you go into the specialty of colorectal surgery?" I have to honestly admit, "When they said 18 holes a day, I thought they meant golf."

The down side is that, as a board certified colorectal surgeon, they only let me play golf on the "rear nine"!

You know it is going to be a bad day on the golf course when you lose your first golf ball in the ball washer on hole number one.

The other day I was playing golf and I hit my ball into the sand trap. I then asked my caddy, "What should I take into the sand trap?" He replied, "The way you play golf Doc, you should take food and water!"

I looked toward green and then asked my caddy, Do you think I can get there with a 5 iron? My caddy answered… Yes, eventually.

What are the 5 words you never want to hear after you've hit your first putt? Hit again, you're still away.

Golf balls are like eggs – they are small, white, and round, and they come in a box of a dozen. Then, after about 3 days, you have to go out and buy another dozen!

Golfers should always carry two pairs of shorts. Just in case they get a hole in one.

If you think it's difficult to meet some new people on the golf course… Just pick up the wrong golf ball!

The golf pro told me, "Doc, your trouble is that you're not addressing the ball correctly." I replied, "I don't think so because I speak very politely to that golf ball and he's still trying to go hide in the woods!"

These school jokes are really silly! ➡

Chapter 9 – School Jokes

What does Mama Buffalo say to her son every day when he leaves for school? Bison.

The only A's I got when I was in high school were the ones that stood for <u>A</u>bsent.

I asked my third grade teacher why I had the biggest feet in our third grade class. She informed me it was because I was 19 years old.

There was a "kidnapping" at school, so his teacher went and woke him up.

The teacher asked the student, "What is your favorite book?" The student promptly replied, "My parent's check book."

The teacher had to tell one student that his grades were like the "Titanic." They were all below "C" level.

What did the English book say to the Math book? You've got way too many problems.

If sleep is really good so for your brain, why won't they let us do it in school?

The Mom asked her daughter, "What did you learn in school today?" The daughter replied, "apparently not enough... I have to go back again tomorrow."

The numbers had a meeting at school. As usual, the number zero was late for the meeting. When the number zero walked in, he looked over at the number eight and said, "Nice belt."

Why is the word "level" the easiest word to get right in spelling class? Because you can spell it frontward or backward and still get it right.

What did the triangle say to the circle in geometry class? You just don't get the point.

Sammy in geometry class.

Chapter 10 – Farm, Cow, and Food Jokes

Farm and Cow Jokes

The farmer's cow just had her baby. She was "decaffeinated."

What do call a bull sleeping in the field? A "bull dozer."

How do you stop a bull from charging? Take away his credit card.

What did the trailer ask the tractor? "Is that you, John Deere?"

The tractor then looked back at the trailer and said, "I think we ought to get hitched."

Why did the cow cross the road? To get to the "udder" side.

What do you get from a cow with a bad memory? Milk of Amnesia.

What do you call a cow that doesn't give milk? A "Milk Dud"

Why do cows look up to the sky at night? They hope to see the Milky Way.

A horse ran away from the farm and walked into a bar. The bartender took one look at him and asked, "Why the long face?"

Why shouldn't ponies give speeches? Because they are a little "hoarse."

What do you call a cow with no legs? Ground beef.

What do you call a cow with only two legs? Lean beef.

What do you get when a chicken lays an egg at the top of the hill? An egg role.

Why does a chicken coupe have 2 doors? If it had 4 doors, it would be a chicken sedan.

What do you get from pampered cows? Spoiled milk.

What did Mama Cow say to Baby Cow? Get to bed… it's "pasture" bedtime.

Food Jokes

What kind of fish goes best with your peanut butter? Jellyfish.

I won't tell you my silly peanut butter joke because I'm afraid you will spread it around.

When should you go on red and stop on green? When you are eating watermelon.

Why was the tomato blushing? Because he saw the salad dressing.

Don't you dare steal my block of cheddar cheese, because it's "Nacho" cheese.

The banana would not go outside on the sunny day because he was afraid he might peel.

I told one of my bad groaner jokes to a dozen eggs and they all "cracked" up.

Last Thanksgiving one child told his mother that his turkey really had a "fowl" taste.

What did Baby Corn ask his Mother, Mama Corn? Mommy, where is Pop Corn?

I went to pick up my carry-out pizza and asked, "Will my pizza be long?" The take-out clerk politely answered, "No sir, it will be round."

The baby strawberry was very upset when he found out his mother was in a jam.

A cow survived a hurricane. When they milked her the next day they got a milkshake.

What is the name of the Mexican National Telephone Company? Taco Bell.

Chapter 11 – Post Office and Letter Jokes

What eight letter word really only has one letter contained in it? Envelope.

The post card advised the stamp, "Just stick with me and we'll go places." The stamp then replied, "You know I will, because I've really become attached to you."

I told a postman that telling jokes is a lot like the postal service. It's all in the "delivery."

I bought a special stamp at the post office for a package and asked the postal worker, "Should I stick it on myself?" The postal worker politely replied, "It will get there quicker if you stick it on the package."

Did you hear the one about the envelope that had no stamp? You wouldn't get it.

Why shouldn't you stamp your emails? Because your foot would smash your laptop.

What two words have thousands of letters in them? Post Office.

If your girl friend returns all your letters as "second class male", you are in deep trouble.

The girl snake sent a letter to her boyfriend snake and signed it, "With love and hisses."

How do skeletons send letters to each other? They prefer to use the "Bony Express."

What letters are not in the alphabet? The ones in your mail box.

Be aware that "The Alphabet" only has eleven letters. "The Alphabet" (count 'em - 11 letters)

Chapter 12 – Wedding and Spouse Jokes

The husband asked his wife if she ever fantasized about him. She said yes, she often fantasizes about him taking out the trash, mowing the lawn, and occasionally helping to do the dishes.

The best way to remember your wife's birthday is to forget it just once.

The husband really goofed up and he forgot their first wedding anniversary, so, his wife tells him: "Tomorrow morning, when I get up, you'd better have something out in our driveway for me that goes from zero to 100 in less than 6 seconds." So, the next morning, she gets up, goes out to the driveway, and there she finds a bathroom scale… He is expected to get out of Intensive Care soon and perhaps make a full recovery.

Two car radio antennas were next to each other in the parking lot. They fell in love and they decided to get married. The wedding wasn't all that much, but the reception was great!

Two spiders decided to get engaged, after they recently met on the "web."

What's the difference between the boyfriend who becomes her husband? Usually about 30 pounds.

The very wise husband only argues with his wife when she is not around.

The lady should never marry a man to reform him – that's what reform schools are for.

What do you call a woman who knows where her husband is every night? A widow.

Why did the bee decide to get married? Because he found his "honey."

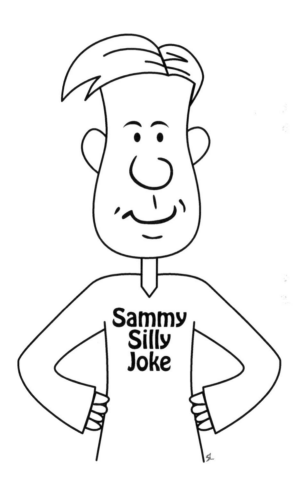

About Your Author – James A. Surrell, M.D.

Fellow, American Society of Colon and Rectal Surgeons (ASCRS)
Fellow, American College of Surgeons (ACS)

Dr. Surrell is a board-certified colorectal surgeon and holds fellowship status in both the American Society of Colon and Rectal Surgeons and the American College of Surgeons. He devoted 14 years to formal education with 4 years of pre-med at Northern Michigan University, 4 years of medical school at Michigan State University, 5 years of general surgery residency and one year of colorectal surgery fellowship. In addition to the best-selling *SOS (Stop Only Sugar) Diet* book, Dr. Surrell has authored many articles in various medical journals on topics related to his specialty of colorectal surgery and digestive health. He is also the author of the personal motivation book, *The ABC's For Success in All We Do* and the digestive health book, *Your Human Digestive System Owner's Manual.*

Dr. Jim, or "Doc" (as he prefers to be called) is also a much sought-after speaker and speaks frequently to local, regional, and national public and professional groups. He blends a significant amount of humor into his many talks and is generally available to speak to nearly any group with an interest in learning more about various topics, including: digestive health, diet and weight loss, cholesterol reduction, healthy nutrition, cancer prevention, and other healthy lifestyle topics. He also appears frequently on various TV programs, and writes a very popular Marquette Mining Journal newspaper column entitled: "Talk with the Doc."

Here is Dr. Surrell's favorite quote:
"There isn't much humor in medicine, but there is a lot of medicine in humor."

64389866R00031

Made in the USA
Middletown, DE
03 September 2019